CW00420736

THE ORB REPORT

A collection of quirky sci-fi short stories

Kris Derry

STORIES ...

Preface

Welcome to a bizarre and fascinating collection of sci-fi short stories, covering a variety of concepts that include robots, time travel, retro-futurism, cyberpunk, virtual reality and deep space exploration.

Intriguing, eclectic, and chiefly characterised by a not so inconsiderable number of ending twists ranging in style from banal clichéd groaners to surprise thought-provokers to flat-out sardonic nihilism.

Some of these stories could also be classified as parody, but the kind light-hearted flattering type, not the pointy finger mocking type.

So pull yourself up by your bootstraps, fasten your anti-gravity belts and prepare your optical implants for a dazzling array of quirky, offbeat and occasionally surreal sci-fi short stories. Featuring malfunctioning portals, rick rolling robot butlers, entire planetary body counts and bewildered time travellers ...

JETS AND ROCKETS

It was a retro-futuristic jet age. Most people's habitats were floating tens of metres above the ground suspended by an array of auxiliary lift jets. There was an intricate network of tubes twisting through the air, semi-translucent and colour coded to indicate the transportation of various items, including humans.

The sky was always blue, even metaphorically, everything was impeccably swish.

Our story starts with a written note arriving at the Zaxxon residence via the orange tube. It was addressed to Synthia who retrieved it and read, 'It's so on today, bring the jetpacks.'

"Epicness!" Synthia said out loud to herself.

"Homebot! Where's Keef?! I need him to get ready!" she called to the autohelp.

"He's trying to put his jetpants on over his rocketboots again," came the reply.

The End

HYPERFAST TRAVEL

In a massive universe populated with such amazingly bizarre and wonderfully diverse lifeforms someone somewhere was bound to do it sooner or later. In the end, it was the infinity-brained fractaloids of Zoopfroodal 4 who accomplished it.

This invention was a patented device known as the inconceivability drive, which enabled the travelling of any pre-calculated trans-universal distance to occur in mere seconds.

Everyone whooped with joy, especially the inter-galactic travel agents. The barriers across space were effectively gone.

The only beings uncomfortable with this were the super-intelligent potatoes of Froontuber 3, mainly because the sentient potato peelers of Zenarrex 5 had been after this particular technology for ages.

The End

DREAM OF REALITY

The world was disintegrating around him - It was a world of advanced tech, conapts and simulacrums. Just now it was transforming and melting as if he had unknowingly ingested some high quality hallucinogenic compound. The worst part of it was his growing paranoia about the over-state, but then this was only one of the layers of reality pervading his already fractured perception.

He would sometimes sit there at night vividly recalling events from his past, but now, how could he trust his own memories as the over-state had the power to erase and implant new ones? He didn't even know if he was the same person he was half an hour ago.

Staring through the plexi-viewport the world outside appeared desolate, like it had been nuked. Juxtaposed with this was another world, a natural world, pure and uncontaminated. Yet, even *those* were most likely illusions with the real world being just out of grasp, elusive and indeterminate. A capricious blur between the layers.

There was a growing awareness now that he wasn't alone. A figure in the room slowly came into focus... She was wearing a dark polychrome uniform with a black helmet, its darkened visor half raised.

He studied her for a moment.

Her overall appearance and demeanour was definitely military in style.

"What's my role here again?" he asked cautiously, trying not to give away his present state of schizo-confusion.

"You are the over-leader of the over-state," came the tort reply.

"Right," he said, "We've got a helluva job to do then."

The End

MARTIAN WATER

The year was 1895.

The brass spaceship percolated steadily on its way to Mars venting a brief trail of evaporating bubbles in its wake. A crew of three were attentively manning the various levers, wheels and knobs that operated the pistons and assorted steam contraptions.

Captain Will Von Williamson was at the helm. He leaned over to peer through the small glass portal, and while stroking his luxurious moustache he commented, "There she is, straight ahead. Shouldn't be too long now gentlemen."

The first officer Sam Von Samuelson said, "Thank goodness! I'm a touch parched to be frank. Our ship's supply of drinking water is running low. I sincerely hope there's enough water on Mars for us when we arrive there."

The Captain spoke in his congenial and assured

manner, "Don't worry Number One, our top science experts and astronomers inform us there's an intricate network of canals and possibly even lakes on Mars. Once we land we can refill all our flasks and beakers."

After a short pause he added, "And if you've brought your bathing suits we may possibly go for a quick paddle too."

The End

FIRST TIME VOYAGER

part 1

The neon hoop crackled, spitting out liquid sparks like an extravagant firework. Sam Marz could almost smell the air of the twenty-fifth century filtering through the shimmering portal ahead of him.

Filled with an heady mixture of excitement and apprehension he flipped the final switch for the first time.. It was ready.

He stepped through.

Zzzipp.

"Sam Marz!" an assertive voice cut through the air abruptly from behind him. Startled, he spun around to see where the voice was coming from. It took him maybe a couple of seconds to gather his bearings. He hadn't been at all certain of the physical side effects of traversing almost three centuries instantaneously, but he seemed okay, faculties and sensibilities all in one piece.

There, standing in front of him was a smartly dressed individual with large lapels sporting numerous insignia that gave a measurable appearance of importance.

"Hello?" Sam enquired.

"My name is Freddarz, I'm your point of contact for your future-historic first time journey. My role is primarily to help with your orientation into the twenty-fifth century. You'll require an extensive debriefing regarding the customs and protocols of this time period. Please follow me," said the individual, motioning towards a brightly lit exit.

"Oh? Excellent. Thanks." Sam wasn't really expecting a welcoming party, albeit a party of one. He pondered momentarily on the nature of deterministic temporal mechanics, and wondered if his arrival had already happened retrospectively, as it were. So this event had been recorded and received through some kind of time transmission from even further in the future, in which case whatever he was about to do would also already be absolute history. After quickly convincing himself he still had a modicum of free will and determinism, he duly followed Freddarz.

Upon reaching the other side of the exit they stopped.

"Before we proceed to the outer tubes we will require the vitamin shower," Freddarz indicated the nozzles embedded in the ceiling.

"Sure," Sam said going with it, and then with an afterthought, "Exactly what vitamins are they? If you don't mind me asking?"

"I honestly don't know," Freddarz admitted, "No one really asks. Let's just say they are *Earth-state* approved vitamins."

"But.. but.." Sam protested, he was visibly reluctant to go any further.

"I know what you're thinking," Freddarz said, reassuringly, "Allow me to put any concerns you have at ease. If these vitamins were in any way bad for us we'd all be dead by now, judging by the number of times everyone here has been subjected to this type of routine."

Freddarz proceeded to stand directly under the nearest nozzle.

A fine mist emitted.

Astonishingly Freddarz then died.

The End

THE PROTAGONIST

Our story opens with the protagonist performing incredibly heroic deeds. It is the year 2275 and certain people are falling victim to the antagonist, an inter-dimensional villainous rogue who appears to be a highly trained laser-bomb expert. The kind of villain who endears himself to the audience due to the fact his character is complex and infinitely more interesting than our hero. After some detective work and a multi-dimensional chase sequence, our protagonist has the villain within reach. Suddenly the hero is experiencing an internal conflict as the antagonist has been shown to be targeting only bad people. Resolving this issue and disposing of the villain the protagonist's story arc is now complete, simultaneously increasing the hero's interest factor.

The End

SPACEPORT

In the platinum age of interstellar travel, before teleportation was perfected, people were required to go through security checks at the spaceports. A process not unlike the passport control customs of the ancients where people used to queue for hours to be scrutinised, and occasionally searched.

Bodroz was in such a place. He had just disembarked from the EasyPlasma craft that had carried him the eighty-one light years on an economy priced ticket and was now queueing up with the other passengers.

He noticed the guy in front had more than the regulated amount of hand luggage and momentarily wondered how he was able to get away with that, until on further inspection he noticed the guy had four arms. Ah, he thought, if only I'd sprouted an extra arm before my holiday, I could have increased my hand luggage allowance too.

Hand luggage was more vital than ever in the years of public space travel, sometimes you just weren't guaranteed your suitcases would arrive at the correct planet. For Bodroz, a previous experience had seen his luggage not only arrive at the wrong moon, it had ended up in entirely the wrong solar system altogether.

An hour later he was at the security desk.

"Business or pleasure?" asked the official swiping through Bodroz's passport stats on her holo-screen.

"Pleasure," Bodroz said, sporting a genuinely enthusiastic grin.

The official narrowed her eyes, clearly she had taken an instant dislike to him. She slapped the purple button. A booth to the side lit up.

"If you'd like to step this way sir," she said, "We'll need to conduct some routine security checks."

Bodroz followed her into the booth. Maybe it was the Algoluvian infestation I contracted on Zeta Persei that showed up on my records? he wondered to himself. They could be pretty tough on the old bacteria thing.

Once inside the booth he found two security agents already rummaging through his bags.

One of them asked, "Have you brought any strange fruit or vegetables with you?"

"No.. Why, would you like some?" Bodroz quipped, trying to lighten the mood.

Unimpressed by his flippancy they carried on searching. Finding nothing of interest in his belongings they moved on to their next phase.

"You'll now be required to undergo a non-invasive body search."

They handed him a list of procedures which included swabs from all three of his armpits, nail clippings and scrapings from under his toenails, a swab of his nasal mucous, some arterial blood, a sample of his brain tissue, three pubic hairs and an anal probe.

Bodroz shrugged, and wondered what the invasive version would be like.

The End

THE PROTAGONIST 2

Due to the unmitigated success of the first story a sequel was commissioned. This time our protagonist is up against a rogue team of mad physicists whose evil plans involve detonating a matter phase transition super-bomb that will alter the quantum nature of the entire known universe. While infiltrating their lab our hero is caught by this team but manages to foil their plot due to the team leading physics professor gloating for too long in a manner typical of antagonists.

With nano seconds to spare the bomb is diffused and the universe is safe once again.

In the closing chapter though, one of the mad scientists manages to escape and vows revenge, setting up a further sequel whilst increasing the potential for a franchise.

The End

THE LAST WORD

The students filed into the auditorium for the first lecture of the day, holo-notepads with gesture personalisations at the ready.

The 3D A.I. professor flickered on, modelled on a stern looking school ma'am. She cast a scrutinising eye over the class, she waited for everyone to settle, and when they were all focussed towards her she began.

"Welcome all." This produced an amount of tittering, murmuring, and mild surprise. She continued, unfazed, "Today's topic is a brief history of spoken sentence truncation, using the older language style for perspective." A relaxed mood then swept through the hall.

"During the last three hundred years words started vanishing from the ends of phrases. These words were considered superfluous, especially if used in familiar phrases. This started towards the end of the twenty-first century and is still progressing today.

"For an example let's look at the phrase 'We're all going on a summer holiday'. The first iteration became 'We're all going on a summer..' because everyone knew what that last word was going to be. It then became 'We're all going on a..' again, expectation filled the gap. A few more decades passed and the expression turned into 'We're all going..'

"Now, this trend for sentence shortening continued to our current era. Can everyone tell me what this particular phrase is these days?"

The students were silent.

The lecturer wordlessly confirmed they were correct.

The End

PLANET IN PERIL

Their planet was in the throws of a total breakdown. A real geological catastrophe, seemingly caused by an errant black hole that had been 'kicked out' of a twin orbit light years away and had recently zoomed by their heliosphere making a complete mess of all the orbital resonances in their solar system.

The inhabiting humanoids gathered their top experts for a groupthink conference on how best to deal with this impending disaster. The most popular suggestion was to relocate to another planet. Their technology hadn't really advanced to this stage, but with the right funding and an enormous drive involving the smartest scientists it seemed at least plausible, if not the best option. Until the people who voted for this were suddenly cancelled for holding the wrong opinion - something to do with unacceptable risk standards involving potential loss of lives.

The winning plan came from a minority of experts who declared themselves as an overwhelming majority, mainly because they'd bullied everyone else out of their positions. This plan was audacious though. They were to use a planet-wide geo-engineering program to elicit the aid of passing aliens by writing the word 'HELP!' in massive letters using visible particles in the upper atmosphere, so large it could be seen from space.

This they accomplished and then sat back and waited for help to arrive.

After a little while they all perished...

Ironically, there were some aliens that had flown by, but because the inhabitants of the dying planet had not yet made contact with anyone else in that galaxy no other beings had understood their written language.

The End

FIRST TIME VOYAGER

part 2

The neon hoop crackled, spitting out liquid sparks like an extravagant firework. Sam Marz could almost smell the air of the twenty-fifth century filtering through the shimmering portal ahead of him.

Filled with an heady mixture of excitement and apprehension he flipped the final switch for the first time.. It was ready.

He stepped through.

Zzzipp.

Unfortunately he had made an error in his calculations regarding the spatial coordinate temporal mapping system. He found himself in the vacuum that the Earth had occupied two hours previously along its path in space. He was basically in deep space, looking at the

Earth from a distance. This was all academic of course, because presently a great deal of pain was attacking every nerve in his body. Quickly realising his error he employed his suit's inbuilt jets to reverse his momentum and shot back as fast as he could through the still open hoop.

Luckily the whole adventure had only taken about twenty seconds, but it was enough to put him in the medi-bay for a week, where they recalibrated his DNA from the spectrum damage he'd received from cosmic rays.

The recovery period would give him ample time (unironically) to decide whether or not to scrap the project.

Still, somewhere in the back of his mind he couldn't help feeling something odd had happened here, despite his inadvertent mapping blunder.

The End

DOUBLE RHETORIC

She had just finished her live political broadcast on behalf of the Labourcrats. She was supremely good at her job, her speech being beautifully articulate, eloquent and persuasive. In the history of politics she was, without doubt, the most successful candidate ever. The number of shares and loves in the bias bubbles had never been higher.

Striding back to her dress-pod she acknowledged the cheers, praise, and general support from her crew, plus a few random fans that had cunningly made it into the studios to swoon at her.

Back in the pod she removed the blue brain-drive from behind her ear and inserted the red one. She was now ready to carry out a ridiculously successful political broadcast on behalf of the Republitives.

The End

PARADIGM SHIFT

It was a reasonably good gig being a theoretical scientist. The majority of published theories were so mind-bendingly complex that if you wanted to challenge the orthodox viewpoints you were up against some wild and crazy equations that occasionally involved imaginary numbers. You were also fighting people in established positions of authority within their respective fields. These people had lifelong careers built on their work and they'd be fucked if they were going to allow someone younger (or older) and brighter than them to come along and alter the textbooks that they themselves had authored and made a packet out of.

All sorts of dirty tricks were employed by the older, more experienced scientists to prevent these 'upstarts' from gaining any notoriety, or indeed peer review publishing. Most of these tricks also involved some sort of droll insult, usually concerning someone's mother, or at the very least a condescending attitude directed towards them. Very rarely did they involve a structured and articulate debate, as this would be too much of a fair contest.

Kelvin Centigrade was one such challenger. He'd contested the science surrounding the 'Big Bang Theory' which, for centuries after Edwin Hubble had been a lucrative outlet for many scientific careers. His reasoning was as follows; if the expansion of the universe was accelerating then logically if you looked back in time it would be decelerating, and that deceleration would eventually become infinitely slow but never quite reach a zero point. Therefore all time, the universe and everything would have no beginning.

The peer review community responded with, 'When was the last time your mum changed your nappy?'

The End

ADAPTIVE TIME

As with all new technology the military were pretty much always the first to acquire it, and exploit it for their own purposes. They considered themselves privileged pioneers, but in reality they were just guinea pigs constantly under supervision through each level of their hierarchical authoritarian structure.

The time machine was no exception. Once the military had finished whatever it was they needed to do with it the public were then allowed to use it.

Within a matter of days public time travel had solved a long standing mystery, as the public didn't require any level of secrecy clearance and tended to talk a lot about anything and everything.

The mystery was this: the majority of people as they grew older experienced a common sensation of time passing by faster and faster. This was erroneously explained away by suggesting that people's brains became slower with age, producing a false perception of time speeding up, amongst other suggestions. But as soon as people started time travelling they discovered the future people were talking and moving around at much higher speeds than the present. Conversely people in the past were slower. This now, undeniably, explained everyone's sensation of time getting faster. It seemed relative *and* adaptive, i.e. everyone experiences the same micro-acceleration in time and adapts day by day, month by month etc. but journey over a hundred years instantly and the difference in time speed becomes very noticeable.

Though there are those that still claim an alternative theory that says this never used to happen before the military had royally fucked things up with their involvement and initial experiments with this technology.

The End

WIKU

The deep space explorer ship, cheerfully named 'Hi There!', was a reconditioned second class cruiser. It was home to about five hundred humans, all of whom were dedicated to the task of mapping new habitable worlds forming in the stellar nurseries at the points where their home galaxy was intersecting with, or to put it more accurately, capturing another galaxy.

Due to the longevity of the mission a pre-planned breeding program was in place, complete with additional medical filters to prevent the gene pool from degrading. The new baby batches were then subsequently delivered on a precise schedule between hibernation cycles.

Generations later, the most recent group of youngsters from this micro-society had become distinctly bored, with very little motivation for the original purpose of the mission; and despite the constant drip feed of positively reinforced 'exploring is fun' babble perpetually drummed into them from birth, they had developed what was best described as an 'unscheduled' listlessness.

The result of this boredom had lead the kids to invent an exciting new game to play each time they arrived at a new planet. The game was called 'wiku' - an acronym for 'will it kill us'. The rules were quite simple... they would beam down to a new planet's surface and dare each other to eat the first fruit or vegetable they discovered.

The older crew members finally found out about this game and unsurprisingly concluded that it was staggeringly irresponsible. Thus, stringent 'anti-wiku' measures were put in place.

In a semi-ironic twist of fate their dead ship was found floating in space years later after an aggressive assault on the crew from a disgruntled alien community of fruit-based lifeforms.

The End

THE IMPOLITE ROBOT

Beep! .. Cockwomble!! .. Beep!

The End

REWRITING HISTORY

Throughout history changes have occurred, not by careless time travellers, but from every modern prevailing culture that wanted to uphold a new or revised common narrative going forward. This happened with some regularity, occasionally as quickly as within a single generation, other times over the course of centuries, but the guarantee was always a filtered, rewritten history.

A new historical truth group was formed, with the objective of cataloguing these switches in cultural bias that history had apparently delivered. Their mission was carried out with the virtuous and benign intention of providing some kind of ultimate truth regarding past events. Unfortunately, future historians branded this group a bunch of lying fake-news merchants.

The End

FIRST TIME VOYAGER

part 3

The neon hoop crackled, spitting out liquid sparks like an extravagant firework. Sam Marz could almost smell the air of the twenty-fifth century filtering through the shimmering portal ahead of him.

Filled with an heady mixture of excitement and apprehension he flipped the final switch for the first time.. It was ready.

He stepped through.

Zzzipp.

"Sam! Quickly! This way!" were the first words he heard immediately upon his arrival. He was in a dimly lit corridor that seemed to stretch away into the far distance. Two men were there, dressed in dark camouflage, beckoning him with a pronounced sense of urgency, one of them already breaking into a sprint. Sam felt compelled to take off with them. While running down the corridor he tried to clarify what was happening, "What's going on? ..Who are you guys?"

"We'll explain everything once we reach our safe space headquarters," panted one of them.

About two kilometres of slightly curving passageway later and the guys stopped at one of the doors on the left. There was a barely audible unlocking bleep and all three of them went through.

They were in a plain room with a basic table, a couple of chairs, a bright lamp and a toolbox. Sam didn't like the look of it, "Wha..?" he started.

"Relax," said one the guys, "This is an abandoned interrogation room, but rest assured we wont be using it on you."

Sam relaxed a little, he was still gathering his questions regarding this experience.

"For reasons that are about to become apparent we are not going to divulge our real names, let's say I'm Man-one and my friend here is Man-two." Man-one continued, "The world and time you came from was still ostensibly a patriarchal society, despite the clamour for equality from many groups. About a hundred years ago there was a big shift in society which, as a result, became matriarchal. Now, this in itself was a reasonably positive move, or at the very least a sideways move, except not long after this a wave of propaganda lead to a takeover by a far right fascist group of women who now rule the roost, so to speak."

Man-two took over the narrative, "Our futurepast records told us when and where you would arrive so we decided, with, I hasten to add, great personal risk to ourselves to intercept your arrival and whisk you to safety."

Man-one added, "We're essentially part of a men's lib underground resistance group. Does this help answer any of your questions?"

Sam was nonplussed. In fact at that moment he was getting a growing sense of deja vu, but before he could formulate any kind of response there was a loud explosion at the door. Two female figures wearing white uniforms rushed into the room. They both possessed nasty looking handheld weapons and, in an instant, disintegrated Man-one and Man-two.

"Thank you for leading us to this pocket of resistance," one of them said, "Our glorious Queen Bee would now like a word with you."

Sam instinctively kept his mouth shut, but they zapped him with a silencing beam regardless.

The End

LOVELY DAY

It was a beautiful morning, the blue sky was radiating through the window and there was a distant sound of birds tweeting their greetings to the day's start. It was the kind of day that had that air of intangible promise.

This put Hector in a very good mood. He'd recently been working on a vitally important presentation for his company, and today it was ready to roll.

Fully dressed and appropriate hat selected, he made his way to the apartment elevators. A quick descent of seventy-nine floors later and he was out on the city streets.

Today was definitely going to be his day.

He then started off in the direction of his office, the successive waves of his muscular foot leaving a trail of mucous-type slime on the pavement behind him.

The End

VIRTUAL SLEEPWALK

A concerned group had noticed Margery was starting to sleepwalk these last few days, but they couldn't quite agree on whether she was doing it inside the VR with her brain-chip still connected to the headset whilst physically asleep in a resting position, or alternatively, her virtual self had become disconnected from the set and was running its own program based on her personality data sync upload.

The End

INTERSTELLAR TOURISM

The spaceship was nicknamed 'The Gleaming Streak'. One of the first of its kind, with a snazzy integrated reactor and propulsion system, and a range of about 500 parsecs. The passengers were conscious for most of the ship's cruising stage, the rest of the time was spent chemically sedated in the stasis clear goo tanks.

The ship was, at the moment, in cruise mode, almost half way between a duty free spaceport on Phobos and one of the habitable zone exo-moons situated 452 parsecs in the direction of the nearest spiral arm, slightly above the galactic plane.

Dorja was lounging - in the lounge area. Specifically in the section that caters for terrestrial airline nostalgia; complete with tightly packed seat arrangements, an annoying engine hum and the incessant hiss of recirculated air. She removed her headphones. This film is utter shit, she thought to herself, awful plot, terrible acting, no subliminal politics. It was not to her liking.

She then became aware of an eyeball on the end of a slender appendage poking through the seats just to her left from behind. Following the eyeball's gaze she saw the purple being sitting in the adjacent seat, who appeared completely engrossed in a book. Dorja ran a quick discreet scan of the book, the results revealed it to be one of those trashy extra-terrestrial erotic literature titles. Bah, she thought to herself, those books are all slithering tentacles and slimy orifices. It was not to her liking.

"We've only been out of the goo 30 minutes," Dorja said out of the left corner of her upper mouth. The purple being shrugged and the eyeball stayed fixed, unblinking.

Meanwhile, in the navi-control room the pilots

were in a state of panic. They were frantically swiping at map projections while nervously tutting to themselves.

Apparently the ship's star charts bore no resemblance whatsoever to the star positions currently on the live monitors. Something had gone disastrously wrong, presumably during the acceleration stage at the point where everyone was still in the goo.

They were quite lost.

"What about our V.I.P. passenger?" the chief pilot asked, beads of sweat forming on his wrinkling foreheads.

"Dorja?" quizzed the other chief pilot, with an increasing look of horror on her face.

"This definitely won't be to her liking."

The End

INTERGALACTIC TOURISM

"The destination of this intergalactic bus has changed. Please listen out for further announcements."

There were general groans and murmurs of disappointment from the passengers. Then, the second announcement aired.

"Our cabin crew will be along shortly with the in-flight blue pill."

This now prompted collective squeals of delight from everyone.

The End

WELCOME TO 2485

When the 'temporal' travel agent companies produce brochures they are generally out of date by the time the traveller/s reach their destination year. It's one thing to own a time visa, but another thing entirely when the future keeps changing. Take for instance the Barzonko family time trip...

Upon arrival they were welcomed with the fanfare of a cheap sounding downsampled 8-bit trumpet plus holographic confetti.

"Welcome to the year 2485!" chirped the tanned company rep, "If you'd all like to step this way we'll organise your vaccinations."

Mr. Barzonko, clearly confused and a little indignant said, "I'm sorry? My wife, the kids and I have already been vaccinated before we started our journey. What's this now?"

The rep went into full explanation mode, conjuring up a glowing diagram in mid-air,

"Since the time you left, someone from our combined future has jumped back and altered the timeline between your year of departure and the present year. To be more precise it was a time terrorist who set off a type of biological weapon about ninety years ago, changing the atmospheric composition of the entire planet. She somehow managed to evade the time-security task forces, possibly with the use of more advanced time-tech from the future. Every time our teams went back to try and prevent it from happening the attack location changed. They tried over a hundred times and persistently failed. We're now left with a whole spectrum of new diseases that require treatments, especially for those travelling in from past centuries."

The Barzonkos then resigned themselves to having the vaccinations as they didn't want to waste a good holiday.

"So," the rep carried on matter of factly, "the injections we'll give you are just a standard preventative measure to protect you from bacterial, viral, miscellaneous bio-infections and bad ideas,"

"Huh?" said the Barzonko family, in unison.

"As well as immunisation for the new bio-diseases that have sprung up since the attack, you'll all be administered a dose of mind compliance drugs to prevent anti-government ideologies. These enable everyone to think harmoniously as a group, while promoting a very limited ability to question the ruling authority."

Mrs. Barzonko said, "Ah, of course, we have something similar in our time, but since this is the future, I mean *our* future, don't you have more efficient ways of doing these kind of things now?"

"Certainly," came the reply, "That's why these jabs will be done intracranially."

The End

23rd CENTURY COP

He was tough and grizzled. A no nonsense cop. He'd been patrolling Giga-City Seven for a number of years now, which kept him busy and strangely content despite his persistent grimace and emotionless temperament. He liked it best when he was laying down the law in the most brutal manner; the criminals and scumbags deserved nothing less than a solid punch in the face or a random broken bone somewhere.

He arrived home late one day, his uniform slightly torn and stained with the dried blood of deserving criminals when he discovered his wife had bought a delightful surprise for them. It was a cute fluffy puppy. He then spent the next few hours playfully rolling around on the floor with it making 'coochy coochy' noises.

The End

PARKING IN SPACE

Lou-mee was parking her single occupant spacecraft. Today she was meeting with her business associates on Trellox 3 where she intended to discuss a product awareness campaign and negotiate an exciting new deal involving inflatable toenails.

"Vertical drift to level three four three, then proceed to bay eighty," buzzed the comm.

Ah, a doddle here today, she thought to herself, remembering her last stop where she was given a ticket for illegally parking at the wrong Lagrange point. That took a sizeable chunk out of her pay that day. Today's well organised multi-storey spacecraft-park was a delight. Even so, she kept one eye on the console. Her other two eyes were focussed on the naviscreen.

The End

FIRST LIGHT SPEED

The tech was advanced in those days. Not as advanced as warp field mechanics, just fundamentally more advanced than anything preceding it.

The first ever light speed shuttle called 'Flash' was preparing for its maiden voyage. The space agency had completed all of its engineering and calculations months ahead of schedule so now there was just a long ponderous pause before the highly qualified crew were to board for this historic trip. The calculations were the key; Neptune was approximately four light hours away, so if anyone were to view this planet through a telescope they would literally be seeing it as it was four hours in the past, but travel that distance over that time and Neptune would have moved along in its orbit by four hours worth, and would therefore not be in the same position where it was viewed through the telescope. So, for this mission, the correct path to Neptune was factored in with the additional spacetime of about quarter of an hour due to Earth being in conjunction on the other side of the sun. Most people (especially those less familiar with astrophysics) were under the impression that light speed was fairly instantaneous, after all it was exceptionally fast, but to travel vast distances it really wasn't that fast at all. Old science fiction stories would tell tales of hopping from solar system to solar system in a matter of hours by 'jumping' to light speed, but the truth was that even the nearest star to our sun was a little under four whole years away travelling at the speed of light.

The crew were all on board the Flash now, ready for this momentous occasion. All pre-jump checks were complete. Everything was going well. The electromagnetic shield was on - this enabled the relative safety of the ship while travelling at light speed. It was mostly to deflect micrometeorites, but it also kept the shuttle and it's contents safe from the high velocity condensed matter stretch, which was relatively important.

Heading the shuttle crew was Captain Brenda Back, with first mate Doctor Kate Drive, and navigator Ensign Eve Gordon. They were the best of the best. All three of them were exceptionally well qualified with the highest levels of respective skill sets required for the mission.

As the final countdown commenced Mission Control was broadcasting globally with ten billion people currently tuned in. Wishing them luck, and calling them by their space agency shuttle call signs, which in those days was the shuttle name followed by their surname, the speech transmitted through everyone's devices around the planet.

"Good luck to our brilliant and brave light speed heroes: Flash Back, Flash Drive and Flash Gordon!"

And off they went in a flash.

The End

SUPES UP

In the not too distant future genetic enhancements are the norm, not exactly mandatory, but people without these modifications are considered primitive and labelled 'regressives'. The technology behind this advances to such a degree that the modified people are not only given the perfection that previous generations had aspired to but are also gifted with something akin to superpowers. These people are dubbed the 'beyonds'. They have appropriate names to reflect their powers and are chiefly employed to help fight crime.. in a stereotypical manner.

The projected holographic 'Beyonds' signal lights up the sky, and on this particular day IronBalls, GoldenTurd, QuantumFingers and WormholeMoob are ready for action.

The End

FIRST TIME VOYAGER

part 4

The neon hoop crackled, spitting out liquid sparks like an extravagant firework. Sam Marz could almost smell the air of the twenty-fifth century filtering through the shimmering portal ahead of him.

Filled with an heady mixture of excitement and apprehension he flipped the final switch for the first time.. It was ready.

He stepped through.

Zzzipp.

Sam checked his immediate surroundings. Disappointment struck him. He was back in his garage looking at the wall opposite the time portal as if he'd stepped through to his own time from somewhere else.

Something felt different though.

He wandered over to his mirror and studied his reflection. Shockingly he appeared a bit younger than he was earlier that day. He checked his chronometer... Another shock. Almost ten years had passed in his personal time stream.

Scratching his head he tried to consolidate these events into a coherent narrative. I'm ten years older but look younger, he mused to himself. Clearly the machine worked and he had actually gone somewhere, so why had he no memory of the event?

He sat down at his bench and flipped through the holo-manual for the time device. Reading the section entitled 'Paradox Proofing' it said, 'In the extremely unlikely event of a temporal paradox please call this number..' so he called the number, but it was just a recorded message stating, "If the universe around you is still in existence then no harm has been done."

No real help there then.

The End

IMPLANT GLITCH

Zarkron was behaving very strangely.

His friends watched with growing concern as he licked all the door handles whilst claiming to be Emperor of the third moon of Zorp.

"Shit!" said one of his friends, "His neuronic implant is malfunctioning again."

The End

NEIGHBOURS

Towards the end of one of the galaxy's spiral arms lay two adjacent suns, fairly close to each other in cosmic terms. Both suns had solar systems, and both solar systems had a life bearing planet. In both cases these inhabited worlds orbited along counter-rotational paths on the outermost curves of their respective solar systems and would swing by each other every year (this was about 20 years in Earth time). So once a year they would come into such close proximity that they were able to wave to each other as they were passing by. They would view each other's amiable gestures through their newly invented telescopes, at this point it was the golden age of scientific discovery for both planets. Everything was cool. They had a lot of affection for each other.

Fast forward a few years and the situation was quite different. It could be said that these neighbouring planets had now become polar opposites, politically speaking. The friendly waving had been replaced by obscene hand gestures, and the inhabitants of both worlds were now holding up placards with simple written insults like, 'Your Leader Sucks!' and, 'Just Bend Over For Your Leader Why Don't You?!'

This behaviour was prompted, spurred on and assiduously encouraged by both planets' newsfeed media and celebrity influencers.

Then one year, as the *swing by* time was approaching and one planet's population was busy preparing their usual compulsory demonstration slogans, they had a complete shock when they looked through their telescopes. Their neighbour's world had been turned into a smouldering wasteland, with absolutely no visible signs of life. It was utterly destroyed.

The immediate response was confusion, this was normal considering their subtle dictated programming for voicing their opinions with now no one to aim these at. The confusion then turned to sadness, after all, it wasn't that long ago that both these planets were on extremely friendly terms and most of the older generations still remembered those days with fondness.

Lots of theories were put forward as to why and how this happened, all of them wrong.

Unbeknown to these inhabitants there was a third sun, hidden behind their neighbours' sun, with a world that also swung by their neighbours but at the opposite end of their solar system. It was home to a very aggressive race of mutant cyborg rabbits who didn't care much for the waving or sloganeering or even telescopes, and had simply obliterated their neighbour's entire planet out of shear unadulterated spite.

The End

THE GEOENGINEERS

After centuries of perfecting terraforming and other styles of planetary engineering the Sol System environmentalists finally turned their attention to Venus.

They employed sky filters and ground converters, but every time they came close to creating an Earth-like atmosphere the whole warming process started up again.

After a number of failed attempts they had to concede that it was in fact natural for Venus to be super hot, mainly due to its incredibly slow rotation. Since one daytime on Venus was well over a hundred Earth days long, i.e. the sun would hang there in the Venusian sky for about the length of three Earth months, cooking it to a crisp and causing all sorts of havoc with the weather systems.

So, until they could figure out a way to reverse the slow 'retrograde' sidereal rotation and speed up the day-night cycle Venus was to remain super hot..

..and the Mars based travel agent companies relaxed because Venus wasn't about to take away half their business.

The End

HOTEL ROBOT

TX-53S entered the lobby, hovered towards the reception area and dumped its suitcases in front of the posh chrome desk.

Ding.

The auto-attendant rose out of the desk. "Ah, TX dash 53S, we've been expecting you," it said in its mechanical monotone, "Here's your key-drive. You may go straight up."

Once in the room TX-53S performed a quick self diagnostic. Uh-oh, it thought, and picked up the phone. "Hello? Reception?.. I require ROM service."

The End

VIRTUALLY INFINITE

Frex had just wrapped up his VR game campaign. He was feeling that completion buzz. He said his goodbyes to his circuit-bit friends, removed the goggles and switched them off. He was now back in his apartment. Looking around the place, he instantly knew something wasn't quite right. He reached up and, sure enough, he was still wearing goggles. Carefully and deliberately he took the goggles off again. The same problem. Again and again he took them off, employing a variety of methods just to see if that made any difference. No luck. He had somehow hit upon an infinite virtual world layer application. There was only one solution to this kind of problem; if he couldn't manage to take the goggles off in the real world, it would most certainly mean surgery.

The End

EUGENICS

It was a full century after the great human population reset of 2152 and due to the hideously unfortunate accident at Global-Gen-Labs everybody still looked identical.

The End

FIRST TIME VOYAGER

part 5

The neon hoop crackled, spitting out liquid sparks like an extravagant firework. Sam Marz could almost smell the air of the twenty-fifth century filtering through the shimmering portal ahead of him.

Filled with an heady mixture of excitement and apprehension he flipped the final switch for the first time.. It was ready.

He stepped through.

Zzzipp.

There was a momentary blur then his vision sharpened. Strange looking creatures were standing there before him. They each had four upper limbs and two legs. Large electro-rifles nestled in their upper limbs somewhere, he couldn't quite make it out clearly even after this world had come into focus. Their anatomy just looked ..alien.

They were making strange buzzing and clicking noises. Immediately Sam's collar translation unit bleeped. The unit's voice prompt initialised, "Please wait, new language detected. Searching for available data-pack," there was a brief pause, "Pack found, upload complete."

"Hello?" said Sam, and for good measure, "Who are you guys?"

After these last words Sam felt an odd prickling sensation, almost like paraesthesia, but in this current situation he didn't really have time to analyse why.

One of the beings spoke now, lilting through Sam's translation circuit.

"Greetings Sam Marz. We've been expecting you. No doubt you're a little disorientated, but time is of an essence here and we need you to understand quickly that you are not welcome. Your return trip has been pre-programmed, please step back through your device."

They angled their weapons towards him.

"Wait!" Sam protested, "I need to know who you are and what's happened here. Can you not tell me before I go? I have come a long way after all."

Two of the creatures turned to face each other, they appeared to be communicating with one another but Sam's collar unit was silent, although he did detect a very slight change in the room's air. Oh, he realised, they're communicating with pheromones. This was beyond his translator's ability, and it gave Sam an idea for something to work on once he'd returned. They turned back to face him.

"A quick explanation has been authorised," one of them said, "Approximately a hundred and twenty years ago homo sapiens were running genetic experiments on a variety of species and we are the result of one of those experiments. We are, in essence, a hybrid insect race, larger and stronger than humans. Long story short, we became the dominant species on the planet, with the humans now mostly kept in comfortable zoo-like environments."

Sam, clearly astounded, and still wary of the

rifles pointing his way said, "But, aren't you afraid of ..?"

His collar unit crackled loudly.

"Sam, we know the question you're about to ask. We have studied your anomalous time jumps and have decided you're no threat to our existence," after hearing this part, Sam wondered if they were referring to the subsequent time journeys he will no doubt embark upon. The insectoid continued, "You will most likely not remember these events as they haven't happened yet in your home year," now that bit really piqued Sam's interest, some weird unexpected time travel repercussion? "..and as a consequence you will not be able to warn the scientific institutions that were responsible for our inevitable rise to power here.. Now it is time for you to leave."

Before Sam could voice another protest one of the rifles discharged in his direction. There was a forceful rush of air and Sam flew backwards through the portal.

The End

GAME SHOW

Roger had found the perfect scam, so he thought. He had managed to program his time machine so that he could materialise at exactly the same point in time as many times as he wanted without duplicating himself. Utilising this temporal loophole he entered a prime channel game show contest where each time he answered incorrectly he would reset his machine and appear again knowing the correct one. He had now progressed to the final round, and after all his hard work he was ready to win the 'golden swag'.

The presenter asked the question. Roger was stunned, it was a different question from the previous loop, then he noticed the presenter was half squinting at him with a wry smile.

"Shit, they're onto me."

The End

BIO-FUTURE

She was walking along the desolate, dusty track that lead to the bio-city. The bio-suit she was wearing provided more than adequate protection against the bio-particles whipping around viciously in the ceaseless bio-winds.
She paused and started fumbling through her suit. She was going to need her bio-pass to enter the bio-dome.

The Bio-End

NOT ANOTHER ONE

He was careful to arrive unseen, a transient glow and a brief discharge of electricity the only telltale sign of his arrival in the twenty-third century suburban sprawl.

He checked his wrist device, it appeared to be malfunctioning. He shook it to make sure.

Blast, when am I? he pondered. Spotting a person a little way ahead he decided to ask them the obvious question, concealing his twenty-fifth century technology en route.

"Excuse me. What year is this?" he politely asked the stranger.

The stranger stopped, frowned, then touched his earlobe communicator. "Boss! We have another time travelling nincompoop here!"

The traveller was stunned, "How did you ..?"

"Time travellers are the only ones who ask that question, you nincompoop!"

The End

KARMA

There was no proof of the existence of a universal 'spiritual' justice system, but most people loved to believe in this concept as it brought not just hope but also joy - the kind of joy you feel when you see someone who has caused harm come to harm themself. The reason it didn't exist was fairly obvious, most people engaged in what was normally considered bad behaviour would simply get away with it, repeatedly. But occasionally, actually progressively more often as the physical universe became more complex, there would be a coincidental, and satisfying moment of justice...

Armstring was an alien-meat specialist.
Incredibly illegal and extremely immoral, he managed a niche market for those nasty culinary delights.
He had numerous underhanded connections

with the space-fisheries, the stellar alpha sector kennels, and even the military who were, in their own merciless manner, going around removing 'inconvenient' species from newly discovered planets to make way for human colonisation.

He'd fast built up a little empire for people with a taste for this black market food... The real irony here is that humans already had the 3D printing technology to run off any types of organ using template DNA. But his customers were unscrupulous and clearly fancied the real deal.

At the height of his so-called success his operation was infiltrated by an alien animal activist group and he subsequently found himself waking up tied to a bench in a cold store somewhere on Triton.

As he regained consciousness he lifted his head and immediately started to panic.

There it was, an alien, purposefully walking towards him holding a cooking implement.

The End

THE BEAMERS

A group of drunk guys decided on a fun plan to fake a UFO photo. They made their way to a slightly wooded area of a nearby farm, sprayed a plastic frisbee with silver paint, then tossed it into the air, cameras at the ready.

Before they could take the first photo one of them noticed a pulsating red light in the sky, pointed it out to the others and they all stood there transfixed wondering what it was.
Suddenly, all of them were beamed up, experimented on, and placed back in their homes with no memory of the experience.

The following day they all got drunk and decided on a fun plan to fake a UFO photo.

The End

FUTUREBAIT

You'll not believe what the near future has in store for us...

'Clickbait' became the standardised method of communication; every form of spoken or written language was replete with this style of insidious attention grabbing, or, as the stakeholders would call it, marvellous core strategy.

Her intercom buzzed.
The delivery person called out, "Intriguing parcel for you to sign for!"
After accepting the box she opened it.
"Oh my goodness!" she gasped as the light from the box interior illuminated her face.
Nothing prepared her for what happened next...

The End

THE PROTAGONIST 3

Unfortunately due to the noticeable lack of character development for our hero in the second story, plus a lengthy period of what can only be described as 'production hell', the series was cancelled.

Hardcore fans complained and attempted to fund a continuation, but nothing came of it. So it was relegated to the prestigious realm of cult classics.

The End

FIRST TIME VOYAGER

part 6

The neon hoop crackled, spitting out liquid sparks like an extravagant firework. Sam Marz could almost smell the air of the twenty-fifth century filtering through the shimmering portal ahead of him.

Filled with an heady mixture of excitement and apprehension he flipped the final switch for the first time.. It was ready.

But before he stepped through he noticed an object materialising in the middle of the hoop's membrane. He reached forward and grabbed it. It was a book, not like the usual holographic types of the twenty-second century but an old fashioned paper bound book. He studied the title, 'Sam Marz An Autobiography', with a sub-heading that read, 'A warning for all D.I.Y. time machine enthusiasts'.

How is this possible? he thought to himself, I haven't even made my first time journey yet. He switched the time portal off and looked around his garage for his libre-scanner, the book would be far easier to read as an ambient projection.

After he'd finished reading his 'own' book he was rather bewildered.
So, I've been making what appeared to me as first time journey jumps over a hundred times, and each time I travel I hit the future of a random parallel potential? Interesting, he thought.
In the book's glossary was a schematic diagram for an attachment to his machine that would counteract issues such as the origin loop and the future memory problem. This would enable him to immediately recall every trip he's made thus far. He wasn't really at all certain whether he wanted those memories. Many of the adventures he'd apparently experienced seemed fairly unpleasant, plus, if each future he visited extruded differently from the present

what exactly would be the point if he couldn't travel to reconnect with the same place?

Perhaps it's better to ignore my own advice from my own book and just continue travelling first time jumps? he pondered, weighing up the pros and cons of such a decision.

He opened a desk drawer to tidy away the new 'physical' book he'd acquired and was amazed to find a copy of the exact same book already in the drawer.

Now this was an interesting development. He took it out and had a quick flick through it to check for discrepancies between the two copies. They were identical.

So, in at least another one of my resets, he reasoned, I've received this and I must have decided to ignore it, otherwise I'd have remembered it. Oh, wait, after a reset it shouldn't be here at all, plus the book didn't mention multiple versions of my future self sending the same book back.

He drew a conclusion.

The books came from one of my potential futures that is now presenting a subset origin reset of its own... Plus, I have no idea whether I've experienced every single one of those journeys catalogued in my book, therefore I would definitely cause a paradox if hooked up the future memory solution right now. I'll simply carry on with my first time jump.

He switched the portal back on and stepped through, for the first time.

Zzzipp!

"Sam Marz! we've been expecting you!"...

The End
(for the first time)

A LACK OF NIGHT

Civilisation emerged in a triple star system on a planet that was, by a shear fluke of celestial formation, constantly orbiting between at least two suns at any one time. As a consequence they had never experienced a night-time. This lead to their society evolving with no physical (or indeed philosophical) concepts of duality.

So, to summarise - they had no day and night, no war and peace, no yin and yang, no positive and negative, no joy and sadness, no good and evil, no male and female, no life and death, no dual purpose chamfered/bullnose pine skirting, and definitely no beginning and no end...

The End

INTELLIGENT LIFE

Some extra terrestrials classed as witless morons on their own worlds are still more intelligent than the brightest humans on Earth.

The End

EIGHTIES HOBO

It was sometime in the mid-eighties; the land of stonewashed pleated jeans, shoulder pads, aviator sunglasses and big moussed-up hair.

Two friends were on their way to a café to discuss the evening ahead of them. Their plan was to gather a group of mates together to go to a gig at a pub venue near the town centre that evening where a local band was playing. As they were walking along they noticed a weird scruffy guy heading their way. He was dressed in what appeared to be dishevelled grey fatigues that had numerous rips, tears and holes in it. Now, in the eighties this was not as unusual as it seemed, but this guy also had no shoes, was shouting incoherently to himself, had a strange looking rectangular earring and a bar code tattooed on his neck. He basically looked a bit weird.

The two friends immediately avoided his gaze, and with a quick glance at one another they silently decided to cross the street to avoid him. Once the guy had continued on enough they commented to each other along the lines of, "Hobo nutter."

*   *   *   *   *

The 'hobo nutter' was nothing of the sort. His designation was Alek5 and he was part of a thirtieth century elite force division specialising in historical modifications. The reason he was incoherent was due to language evolution - i.e. it is estimated that if a person time travels more than five hundred years into the past, or the future, the native language of the destination year will have 'evolved' away from the year of origin by such a degree that it becomes mostly incomprehensible.

His earring was in fact a wireless temporal communicator device, and he was shouting at his boss.. because shouting is the only language bosses understand.

The End

ANTI-GRAVITY BELT

Rodwin was a bit shifty, always acquiring advanced tech to sell for extortionate prices to the chav-tech citizens, and other such dubious schemes. Today, though, he felt he'd hit the proverbial jackpot. Upon finding a still functioning abandoned temporal portal he'd managed to retrieve an anti-gravity belt from the future. The Floatamatic 5000.

This'll make me a pack of creds, he thought to himself, shiftily. He tried it on and hit the big green button.

Instantly he crumpled into something that resembled a human pancake, due to the fact that the belt's previous owner had left it on a setting for use in an ultra-high orbit planetfall exercise, essentially requiring the belt to be set at thirty times the normal gravity strength.

The End

GOLD PLANETOID

A few hundred years ago the deep space observational instruments were advanced enough to detect exoplanets, and even exomoons that were located half way across the galaxy. One day these observations had detected a planetoid that appeared to have an entire crust made of gold. This type of phenomena had already been theorised as a possibility, mostly within the blast radii of kilonovas, but other lesser understood factors were suspected, due to the abundance of heavier elements detected across the cosmos.

Needless to say this caught the attention of every greedy person on the planet. Entire nations started their territorial disputes and dubious claims regarding this precious find.

This was a shame because the human race had only just figured out the way to a happy and peaceful existence was to eliminate all concepts of ownership and hierarchy, and so the appearance of unprecedented amounts of this rare metal had knocked them back centuries into devolved states of tribalism and feudalism.

It was the twenty-eighth century and the teleships (spaceships capable of repeatedly teleporting across colossal distances) were on their way there now. Three of them, representing the three tribes of the major continents, all the while squabbling with each other about who has the right to more of the gold.

When they arrived they were disappointed to discover they weren't the first ones there (predictably). A familiar looking flag was already planted and flapping in the breeze on the lush golden landscape. It was Antarctica, the fourth tribe. The Antarcticans had somehow gained the technology to travel faster than everyone else a few years before. So the three quarrelling tribes, now unified against their common enemy, were plotting together on how best to engineer a war and steal the gold from them. The sort of thing that was common practice among primitive warring cultures.

The war raged on for decades, many lives were lost and many people were sucked in by the hatred-programming propaganda etc. Finally common sense kicked in, there was enough gold for everyone to share equally, plus, with so much gold about now its value had declined massively, making their fighting appear pointless and ridiculous in retrospect.

Civilisation then settled into a lovely quiet steady phase...

Until their deep space observations detected a planetoid consisting entirely of diamond.

The End

OPAL AND IRON

The suburanic agents had been given an important assignment. There was a spooky hole in the fabric of time allowing spooky entities to travel through as wobbly two dimensional torch lights. These beings then proceeded to cause untold spookiness.

Opal was first on the scene, psy-scanning the area, her photonic crystal eyes glowing nine iridescent colours as she did so. Iron followed up seconds later, a little rusty at the edges but basically tough, and still feeling the self importance of having an entire age named after him.

Utilising their enigmatic skills they were able to remove the batteries from the torches and seal up the anomalous vortex. The spookiness had been averted.

This time..

The End

EIGHTIES HOBO

Epilogue

Alek5 was on the mission. A thousand years from his home time and possibly a little out of his depth. He presumed his boss was testing him by sending him out so far. The photon wars of the twenty seventh century were now looking quite tame in comparison to this task.

There was a band playing tonight and he had to be there to disrupt events, but of course, as with any time altering operation there can be unforeseen consequences in the revised timeline...

The band's name was 'Sage of Great Age', and unknown to them their obscure music was revived by a political faction of the ZeroGen movement in the late thirty second century, with the lyrics from the band's music inspiring a catalogue of unspeakable acts ultimately resulting in the deaths of billions.

The mission was straight forward enough, the lyrics had to be changed. Alek5 would achieve this by befriending the band for a while, in a transient unmemorable manner, (or if they did remember he had a special zapper for that) and use subtle psychology to plant the seeds of a different lyrical narrative that eventually wouldn't be picked up and used in such a horrific way by the ZeroGen-ers.

His entry into the twentieth century had been a bit bumpy.. Not many agents travel more than four or five hundred years as the 'materialise location' becomes increasingly unpredictable. In Alek5's case he'd arrived inside an industrial car crusher, barely making it out okay. He'd lost his shoes and his clothes were a bit torn but his personal body force field had held up sufficiently for him to extract himself without any serious injuries. He felt better after a little rant to his boss about temporal safety measures and a replacement force field.

* * * * *

The mission was successful. He'd even tracked down everyone attending that first gig which included the two guys he'd passed by on the streets earlier that first day - plus their friends - to make sure they couldn't recall the lyrics from that performance.

Now back to his home time to check in with his boss. This time there was no arrival location aberration, luckily enough for him, though he did discover things were a little different. Somehow, the completion of his temporal operation had resulted in himself now being the boss. He sat back in the director's seat and studied the time-grid to make sure the future events had been altered accordingly, which they had. Now he had a decision to make, should he relinquish the boss position? Or just let that slip?

The End

ROLLING GESTURE

Everyone had a robot butler. They'd been present in every home now for a couple of centuries, allowing humans an almost limitless amount of leisure time.

These 'robutlers' were shiny, helpful, self-maintaining and all the bugs had been well and truly ironed out... except one.

The manufacturers had included in the initial design process a command prompted by an unusual body motion gesture that they imagined no one would ever use. And in the final stages of production this had not been removed from the robot's core program.

Unfortunately there was one robutler owner who unwittingly performed this gesture.

The robutler then started singing, "We're no strangers to love .." and never gave up.

♫ The End ♫

THREE BOOTHS

Eztrella had enough holiday creds for her time trip. She sauntered into the yearport, clicked through the flash-scan and followed the glowing dashes on the floor.

She was there now, the Three Booths room.

The first and second booths were marked 'Past' and 'Future' respectively, but she chose the third one, which was labelled 'Lucky Dip'.

The End

UTOPIA

The next best thing happened. Combining all the positive principles of every societal structure into one happy global civilisation, essentially revolutionising the way we revolutionise, and it worked. It was a golden age. Nature was in balance, people were healthy, on the whole no one argued with anyone about anything, the secrets of the universe were unlocked. It was a positive and beautiful time.

There were still small groups of people who objected to this way of life however, mainly claiming, on philosophical grounds, that without negativity the concept of positivity had no meaning. In the interests of perpetuating the wonderful utopian way of life these people were vaporised.

The End

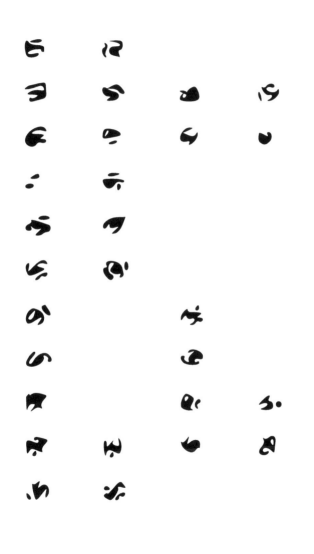

Printed in Great Britain
by Amazon

10864875R00059